Aloha Adventure

By Roger Sipe
Illustrated by Neil Evans

Publishing Credits

Rachelle Cracchiolo, M.S.Ed., *Publisher*
Conni Medina, M.A.Ed., *Editor in Chief*
Nika Fabienke, Ed.D., *Content Director*
Véronique Bos, *Creative Director*
Shaun N. Bernadou, *Art Director*
Carol Huey-Gatewood, M.A.Ed., *Editor*
Valerie Morales, *Associate Editor*
Kevin Pham, *Graphic Designer*

Image Credits

Illustrated by Neil Evans

5301 Oceanus Drive
Huntington Beach, CA 92649-1030
www.tcmpub.com

ISBN 978-1-6449-1315-4

Table of Contents

CHAPTER ONE

Winter of Adventure

I remember that winter, 30 years ago, very clearly. It was the year that my dad grew a beard. "It will be a winter of adventure," he said. But every day was an adventure for us. We lived on the Hawaiian island of Kauai. The tropics never get cold, so we fished, swam, and explored every day.

"This year, we will hike the Kalalau Trail, Daniel," my dad said. I had heard stories about that infamous trail from my best friend's older brother. It was an 11-mile hike across rivers, through jungle, and over a towering sea cliff.

"Are we old enough?" I asked. I was 11 years old, and my brother, Oliver, was only 8. Dad laughed. "We will only hike the first two miles," he said.

We never imagined the true adventure that awaited us!

CHAPTER TWO

Day Trip

"Rise and shine," my dad said quietly the next morning, so as not to wake our mother. "It's time to drive to the trailhead." My brother and I got out of bed and hurriedly dressed. Bacon and eggs were waiting on the table.

We quickly ate and jumped into the jeep with our poi dog, Jackson. Poi dogs are what we call mutts in Hawai'i. We thought Jackson was the cleverest dog in the world. We took him with us just about everywhere we went.

My dad started the engine and told us to buckle up. Our adventure was underway. It was still nighttime, but it wasn't too dark out. We could see stars shining brightly in the early morning sky because there weren't many streetlights to dim them. Oliver and I looked for constellations as the jeep headed north.

CHAPTER THREE

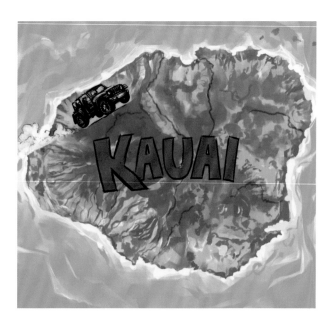

Trail Mix

Frogs were still croaking when we arrived at the trailhead. "The sun will be up soon," my dad said. Before we even began to hike the first section, the sky was getting lighter.

The first mile went up a gradual incline, which was tiring and took lots of steps. However, the path was safe and wide. Up and up we went. Some teenage boys were running the trail and energetically zipped by us.

We reached the trail's highest point at the first mile marker and had a gorgeous view of the blue ocean below. We then began the second mile down to the beach. It was much easier walking downhill! At the trail's end, a deep stream moved rapidly, and a posted sign warned people to watch for flash floods and not to swim in the stream.

We found some long branches and used them as poles to keep our balance as we crossed the stream. My dad had to carry Jackson. Oliver slipped on a small rock and got one shoe wet, but otherwise, we made it across dry. We sat on the beach, had a snack of trail mix, and then hiked toward the waterfall. It was just over a mile and went through an incredible bamboo forest! We arrived at a cool waterfall and the second mile marker.

CHAPTER FOUR

A Little Farther

At the waterfall, my dad got a wild look in his eyes. "Let's keep going up the Kalalau Trail a bit," he said. "We'll just hike up out of the valley. There is another great waterfall just a few miles up, and we can get a great view of the falls from up high."

The next section of the trail was narrow, all uphill, and full of brush and briars. By the time we reached the top, it was starting to get dark quickly. A fast-moving storm was headed our way.

"Oh, no!" my dad exclaimed. He had been so preoccupied with our adventure that he had not noticed the thick, dark clouds moving across the ocean toward us. "If it starts to rain hard, we won't be able to cross the stream to get back."

The wind began to howl. Soon after, sheets of rain began to fall. From our high vantage point, we could see the stream was quickly becoming a raging river. "There's no sense in heading back that way," my dad said. "We will have to get to the ranger station a few miles farther up the trail."

CHAPTER FIVE

◈

Tropical Punch!

It felt like we were in a hurricane—
the wind was fierce, the rain was
torrential, and the trail was muddy.
My dad slipped. His left leg made a
loud and gnarly snapping sound, and
it buckled. He lost his balance and
fell into a 15-foot gully. He cried out

as he crash-landed on a pile of large rocks below.

"Dad, are you okay?" I yelled through the howling wind.

After what seemed like an eternity, I heard a faint reply. "I think my leg is broken," he said in an anguished voice, "and maybe a couple of my ribs are busted. Get help at the ranger station!"

Our adventure was over, and a nightmare was unfolding. Cold, wet, and scared, Oliver and I cautiously made our way up the trail, with Jackson leading the way.

CHAPTER SIX

◈

Seeking Shelter

We knew we had to find the park ranger. Even though we were terrified, we felt confident that help was nearby. After a mile or so through the darkness, we saw a large structure looming in the distance. "It's the ranger station!" Oliver exclaimed. "We're saved!"

As we got closer, though, our hearts sank, as the station was actually a picnic table surrounded by three walls and a roof. Oliver began to cry. I put my arms around him, and tears began to mix with the rain on my face, too. Then, a shadow emerged from behind the shelter.

"Hello, there!" It was one of the teenagers who had run past us earlier that day. He and his cousin were sitting under the structure, trying to stay dry.

We ran to the shelter and told them what had happened.

"You can't go any farther," said the redheaded boy named Kai.

"It's way too dangerous," his older cousin, Andre, agreed. "The next mile, nicknamed Crawler's Ledge, is only six inches wide at some points and more than 500 feet up from the ocean."

"The trail is now a mudslide," Kai said ominously. "One slip could send you to an early grave! We're scared. We're going to wait out the storm here. Once it's over, we will go back the way we came."

Despite Andre's dire warning, I knew I could not stop. I had to find help quickly to save my dad. Someone at the beach would surely know what to do. I left Oliver with the runners. They would double back and try to bring dad up to the shelter. Jackson and I continued on the trail.

CHAPTER SEVEN

Cliff Crawl

As I continued hiking away from the shelter, the path was still slippery and full of puddles. It wasn't much worse than the previous section I had already walked. The beach was miles away, but I was sure I would make it.

Then, the trail came out of the jungle. My jaw dropped and my spine tingled as I saw what was ahead. The trail became pure sludge, hugging a vertical cliff wall. Small waterfalls were cascading down to the ocean, hundreds of feet below.

There was no time to think. I took a deep breath, said a prayer, and started slowly making my way toward Crawler's Ledge. After a few hundred feet, I dropped to my knees. I would certainly have to crawl at this point. But I was frozen with fear and could not move. Now, *I* would also have to be rescued!

Jackson must have sensed my terror. He somehow made his way around me to take the lead. Now in front, he barked until I moved. The trail was very narrow and slick, but Jackson tested every step to make sure it was safe. I mimicked his movements, slowly making it over the steepest point. Back on my feet, I grew more confident with every step. Before long, we were across and back to the jungle. We had survived Crawler's Ledge!

From that point on, it was all downhill—literally! Descending Red Hill was an adventure in itself. The red dirt for which the hill is named was thick, sticky, and wet. It was like walking through glue. I lost both my shoes and had to carry Jackson. I was soaking wet, covered in mud, and barefoot, but I finally made it to the beach!

CHAPTER EIGHT

Sandy Surprise

The storm was now nearing its end, as the wind had stopped and the rain was barely a mist. The campers at Kalalua Beach came out of their tents to see us. We must have looked like two mud-covered monsters heading their way.

"Did you just come across Crawler's Ledge and down Red Hill?" asked one of the campers in disbelief.

"I did," I replied. Through my tears of exhaustion, I told them my story and about my dad's situation.

"We have a radio here at the camp," another camper, named Sandy, assured me. "We will call for a rescue unit ASAP." She was a firefighter and was camping during her vacation. "I was scared hiking that trail in just the sunshine!" she said. "You must be quite the hiker." She put her hand on my shoulder. "Let's get you and your dog cleaned up."

CHAPTER NINE

Air Rescue

Back at the picnic shelter, the rescue went smoothly. Kai and Andre were able to help my dad out of the ravine, but he was not doing very well. The helicopter arrived quickly. It carried a medic, who loaded dad and Oliver onboard. Together, they were flown to the hospital. "It was scary and fun at the same time," Oliver later told me.

I wanted to see my dad, but the helicopter was only allowed to go to places where there was an emergency. I was now safe, warm, and dry on the beach. The storm was over, but the trail was closed. It would take awhile to rebuild the portions that had washed away in the storm. No one would be allowed to hike in or out for days. I was stuck on the beach, or so I thought.

CHAPTER TEN

Ocean Detour

Sandy saw that I was feeling blue. She came over to the campfire I was sitting next to. "Have you and Jackson ever been on a kayak?" she asked, pointing to the ocean. It was fully loaded and ready to go. She said it would only take us a couple of hours to get back to the trailhead.

I put on a life jacket and got into the kayak. Jackson jumped in behind me. Sandy sat behind us, and we pushed off from the beach as the sun began to shine. We had one last adventure as we paddled back. Our ocean route took us along the Kalalau Trail, and from the safety of our boat, the cliffs that I had just crossed mesmerized me. In the distance, a rainbow appeared. It ended at the mainland where my mom was waiting.

CHAPTER ELEVEN

Summer of Adventure?

"Your dad was lucky," the doctor said. "He might have died if he had arrived at the hospital any later. But he'll be back to adventuring in a few months. You are a hero!"

I was not the only one, though. Without Oliver, Kai, and Andre, I wouldn't have been able to find the way

back to the gully where Dad was. The helicopter pilot and medic also braved a terrible storm to help us. And Sandy gave up the rest of her vacation to get me home. We were all heroes. But the biggest hero, in my opinion, was Jackson. His courage on Crawler's Ledge had given me courage.

"You look like you could use a nice reward," my mom said to us. "Let's go get some shave ice from the hospital cafeteria."

Now, that's an adventure I could get behind!

About Us

The Author

Roger Sipe is the former managing editor of *Hawai'i Magazine*. Many years ago, he hiked Kauai's Kalalau Trail by himself and camped at the beach overnight. It was truly a great adventure. He currently lives in Indiana with his wife, two sons—Daniel and Oliver—and a collie named Jackson. Someday soon, he hopes to take his family to Kauai to hike the trail with him…but only the first two miles, of course!

The Illustrator

Neil Evans (aka Nelson Evergreen) lives on the south coast of the UK with his partner, Susannah, and their imaginary cat. He's a comic artist, illustrator, and general all-around doodler of whatever appears in his head. He also makes music and plays lots of video games.